D1112883

For
Thomas and Euan,
my rootin'-tootin' nephews!

PEACHTREE PUBLISHERS
1700 Chattahoochee Avenue
Atlanta, Georgia 30318-2112
www.peachtree-online.com

Text and illustrations © 2013 by Alex T. Smith

First published in Great Britain in 2013 by Hodder Children's Books
First United States version published in 2015 by Peachtree Publishers

Artwork created digitally

Printed in October 2015 by RR Donnelley Asia Printing Solutions Limited in
China
10 9 8 7 6 5 4 3 2 1
First Edition

ISBN 978-1-56145-918-6

Cataloging-in-Publication Data is available from the Library of Congress.

CLAUDE
in the Country

ALEX T. SMITH

PEACHTREE
ATLANTA

Chapter 1

Have you met Claude?

Here he is now.

Hello, Claude!

Beret

Claude

Dashing sweater

Claude is a dog.

Claude is a small dog.

Claude is a small, plump dog who wears a beret and a very dashing sweater.

He lives in a house with his owners,
Mr. and Mrs. Shinyshoes...

…and his best friend, Sir Bobblysock.

Sir Bobblysock is both a sock
and quite bobbly.

When Mr. and Mrs. Shinyshoes
dash out the door to work each
morning, Claude whips out his
beret from under his pillow and
decides what adventure to go on.

Where will Claude and Sir
Bobblysock go today?

Chapter 2

It was Thursday morning and the day before had been a Wednesday. A wet Wednesday. Because their raincoats were still at the dry cleaners, Claude and Sir Bobblysock hadn't been able to go on an adventure. They'd had to stay indoors.

Sir Bobblysock had busied himself writing his life story and Claude had busied himself being bored.

11

First, Claude had thrown himself
down on the carpet and pretended
to be sick until Sir Bobblysock
looked at him and gave him some
attention.

When this didn't work, he did some
running around in circles, watched
a very interesting movie about
cowboys, and gave a concert for
all his other friends. It had been a
rip-roaring success.

CLANG! CLANG! CLANG!

Mr. Smelly Sock

Dr. Chewed Squeakybone

Dame Nibbled-Slipper

←Keith

14

But now it was Thursday and
the sun was out. Claude needed
some fresh air.

"I think I will go to the countryside,"
he said. So that's what he did.

15

Sir Bobblysock thought he might go, too, since he was stuck on a tricky chapter of his book and a day out would do him some good. But he was a little worried about the countryside. He had heard that it was very green. Unfortunately, green was not his best color.

But he decided to be brave and the two friends bustled off.

GRAND THEATER

COUNTRYSIDE

SNOWY MOUNTAINS

It didn't take them long to find the countryside. Claude was surprised by how very big and green it was. Sir Bobblysock realized that he liked it after all.

18

The Countryside

19

There was
plenty to see.

Claude looked
at the grass.

Claude
looked at
the flowers.

And a rather startled rabbit
looked at Claude!

Before very long, Claude smelled a peculiar odor. While it wasn't horrible, it certainly was rather whiffy. It smelled like mud and a little like Sir Bobblysock when he was grumpy and hadn't washed for a week.

WELCOME TO
WOOLLYBOTTOM
FARM

Claude soon discovered
that the smell was coming
from a farm.

23

Chapter 3

He had never been to a farm before, so he decided to go and see what it was like. Sir Bobblysock popped a clothespin on his nose and hopped along behind.

They hadn't gotten very far when a very jolly woman in overalls and boots saw them and started waving.

Claude quickly combed his
ears and Sir Bobblysock
adjusted his bobbles.

"Hello!" cried the woman, marching over to them. "My name is Mrs. Cowpat and I am the farmer here!"

"Hello," said Claude, shaking her hand. "My name is Claude and this is my friend, Sir Bobblysock. May we help you on the farm today?"

COUNTY FAIR
at
WOOLLYBOTTOM FARM
starts at 3pm
CAKE STALLS!
COMPETITIONS!
FUNNY-SHAPED VEGETABLES!

Mrs. Cowpat said, "Yes, of course. I would be glad of the help, since I have a very busy day ahead of me." It turned out that today was the day of the County Fair, when people from all over the place gathered together in the countryside to parade their nice animals around and show each other their funny-shaped vegetables.

Sir Bobblysock liked the sound of that and so did Claude.

"The County Fair takes place in one of my fields this afternoon," explained Mrs. Cowpat. "You two can help me get everything ready!"

She handed Claude a pair of boots and they set off.

Because of all the rain the day before, there were lots of muddy puddles on the farm.

Sir Bobblysock, who on the whole
didn't really like anything grubby,
carefully hopped around them and
was pleased that he hadn't gotten
his bobbles in a mess.

Claude made sure that he splashed
and sploshed in every single one
of them.

32

Some puddles were deeper than
they seemed...

Chapter 4

Their first job was to feed all the chickens and collect the eggs. Claude liked chickens. He liked the way their bottoms wobbled as they walked.

As Claude searched all over the coop for eggs, he practiced walking like a chicken. *Wobble, wobble, wobble* went his bottom. He found that, although he enjoyed it, bottom wobbling was exhausting.

It made Sir Bobblysock
feel dizzy just watching him.

35

Claude was very good at finding
eggs. He had soon gathered a whole
basketful and even found one
hiding under his beret!

"One very important thing I need to do," said Mrs. Cowpat, "is to round up all of my sheep. Usually, I let them go and play in the fields, but today I need to gather them up so they don't make a nuisance of themselves during the County Fair."

Claude and Sir Bobblysock listened very carefully as she explained that she had a special dog called a sheepdog that did all the rounding up for her.

"I blow my whistle," explained Mrs. Cowpat, "and do a bit of pointing and shouting. My dog dashes around the field, gathers all the sheep into a group, and brings them into their barn."

It turned out, however, that Mrs. Cowpat's dog was currently on vacation, so she asked if Claude would do the job for her.

Claude agreed. Sir Bobblysock sat out on account of his stiff knee.

Claude had never been a
sheepdog before. But he found
that he was good at it.

He popped his beret under
his sweater, put on his sweatband,
and jogged all over the fields,
shouting hello and waving
to all the sheep.

Unfortunately, this didn't
round them up. They just
stood and stared at him, wondering
what on earth was going on.

41

Claude decided to try a different approach.

He ran up to the sheep who looked like she was in charge and asked politely if she wouldn't mind going into the barn for the afternoon.

The sheep blushed at being asked so nicely. Then she whistled to her friends and they all trooped into the barn.

"Well done, Claude!" said Mrs. Cowpat when he raced back to her. "You make a wonderful sheepdog!"

Sir Bobblysock beamed with pride.

Chapter 5

Their next job was to take care of the horses. Claude was very excited to see them. All the cowboys in the movie he'd watched the day before had ridden horses and looked very sharp doing so.

"These horses need a bit of exercise," explained Mrs. Cowpat. "Would you like to take them for a ride?"

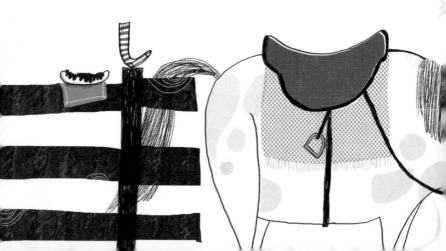

Claude nodded excitedly, but Sir Bobblysock declined. He'd ridden a horse before and it hadn't ended well, so he decided to sit on the fence and have a chocolate éclair instead.

At first, Claude enjoyed his horse
ride and felt just like a cowboy.
He even found a lasso in his
beret, which he waggled above
his head enthusiastically.

Then, unfortunately, the horse got
a bit carried away and Claude
didn't enjoy the ride half as much...

Mrs. Cowpat quickly untangled
Claude and helped him smooth
down his ears, which had gotten all
windswept in the excitement.

"I think we could do with a nice cup of tea and a break," said Mrs. Cowpat. The three farmers shared a thermos of tea and had a slice of fruitcake each.

It was lovely to have a rest for a few minutes and Claude and Sir Bobblysock were just closing their eyes for a moment when…

The biggest rooster you have ever seen crowed in Claude's ear.

It frightened the life out of him and made Sir Bobblysock a nervous wreck. He'd never been one for sudden loud noises. A grasshopper had jumped out at him once— he had taken to his bed for three days with his eye mask on and a *Relaxing Sounds of the Rainforest* CD playing in the background.

Claude didn't want all of that to
happen again, so before the rooster
could make another noise, Claude
threw a big piece of cake into its
mouth and popped a pair of
earmuffs on Sir Bobblysock.

"Let's do something else now," said
Mrs. Cowpat. "Something a bit
calmer perhaps."

Chapter 6

She showed Claude and Sir Bobblysock her haystacks, her cows, her fearsome-looking bull, and lastly, her pigs.

Claude sniffed a big sniffy sniff. *Aha!* he thought. *The pigs smell a little bit like cheesy socks!* And he couldn't help noticing that they were covered in mud and looked very messy indeed.

Mrs. Cowpat suddenly looked at her watch and gasped.

"Oh, my goodness!" she cried. "The County Fair is about to begin and I haven't gotten everything ready. These pigs are competing in the Most Beautiful Pigs competition and look at the state of them! Would you mind giving them a quick wash while I go and check that all the stalls have been set up?"

Claude helped Mrs. Cowpat pull
out a long hose and an old tin bath.

"Thank you," she said, dashing off.
"I'll come back in a few minutes
and see how you are doing."

Claude looked at the mucky pigs.
Then he looked at the old tin bath.
Then he looked at Sir Bobblysock
and Sir Bobblysock looked back at
Claude.

He popped his beret under his
sweater, tied his ears above his
head, pushed his sleeves up, and set
to work.

When Mrs. Cowpat came back, she wasn't at all expecting to see what she saw...

"Oh!" said Mrs. Cowpat.
"They look...err...lovely..."

But she couldn't say any more, as the clock struck three and the County Fair had begun.

61

There was such a lot to see, and an awful lot for Claude and Sir Bobblysock to do.

They sampled the cakes at the cake stall (just in time for their three o'clock snack).

They looked on in amazement while somebody showed off her award-winning pumpkins.

They clapped loudly when a man won a prize for his cucumber.

And they held their breath as a very
snooty-looking man with a
clipboard marched around Mrs.
Cowpat's pigs, judging them in the
Most Beautiful Pigs competition.

Eventually, he scribbled something on his pad and announced that Mrs. Cowpat had won! Claude threw his beret up in the air with excitement.

The snooty judge rolled his eyes and marched off across the field to judge the Most Angry-looking Bull competition.

Chapter 7

Claude and Sir Bobblysock carried on looking around. There was a Most Handsome Dog competition in ten minutes' time. Claude was just deciding whether to enter, when from across the field there came the most dreadful noise.

DANGEROUS BULLS

FUNNY-SHAPED VEGETABLES

CAKE STALLS

ARE YOU A DAPPER DOG? IF SO, THE **MOST** HANDSOME **DOG** COMPETITION IS FOR YOU! 3.30PM TODAY

RRGGGGHHHH!"

Claude and Sir Bobblysock dashed to where the noise was coming from. It didn't take them long to discover what was going on.

The snooty-looking judge had obviously done something to make one of the big bulls very angry and it was now chasing him around the pen. Its big spiky horns were heading straight for the judge's bottom!

"Somebody save him!" cried
Mrs. Cowpat. Nobody knew
what to do.

Just then, Claude had an idea.
He remembered the cowboy movie
he had watched the day before.
Claude pulled his lasso out from
under his beret and strutted into
the ring.

Sir Bobblysock's bobbles shook
with fright and he covered his eyes
(except he couldn't help peeking).

The angry bull was galumphing around like a lunatic, and the poor judge was running as fast as he could to keep out of the way.

"Help!" he shouted.

Claude stood in the middle of the ring and whirled his lasso above his head.

He whirled it and twirled it and twirled it and whirled it.

The judge was still galloping around
the ring with the bull right on his
heels. Suddenly, the judge slipped
on the grass and *whoooooooosh!*

He skidded across the pen and landed—*splat*—face first in a cowpat!

The bull screeched to a halt.
Then, with steam coming from its
nostrils, it started to scrape its
hooves on the ground. *Scrape!*
Scrape! Scrape! Then—*Kaboom!*—
off it went like a bomb.

It ran at full speed, with its head
tucked down and its horns
glinting in the sunshine.
It was just inches from the
judge's bottom when
Claude flung
his lasso up
into the air.

Everything was silent.

Sir Bobblysock could hear his heart
thumping in his chest.

Claude took a deep breath and then...

...when the moment was just right, he flicked his paw and tightened the lasso around one of the bull's horns. He had captured it!

83

Chapter 8

Claude pulled and pulled with all his might, and eventually the bull came to a stop.

He walked up to it with a determined little walk.

"Now," he said, "you are being a very naughty boy!" He wagged a finger at the bull. "Are you going to stop chasing this nice man?"

The bull nodded.

"Good," said Claude, and he reached under his beret and found a cupcake he'd stashed there for emergencies. He gave it to the bull, who nibbled away at it politely.

The crowd that had gathered roared with applause. The judge shook Claude's paw and said, "Thank you." He didn't seem that snooty anymore!

Mrs. Cowpat came running over to Claude, with Sir Bobblysock hopping behind her.

"What a brave dog you are!" she said breathlessly. "I don't suppose you'd like to stay and be a farmer here on my farm, would you? You'd be super!"

Claude thought about it for a minute. He'd had a lovely time—and all the fresh air had certainly put some color in his and Sir Bobblysock's cheeks—but he did like his cozy bed at Mr. and Mrs. Shinyshoes's house.

Claude could see that all that bull business had been a bit too much for Sir Bobblysock. He looked like he needed one of his long naps in a dark room. Claude politely explained all of this to Mrs. Cowpat.

She was a bit disappointed but said that she understood. "You must come back and visit soon," she said.

Then she gave Claude and Sir Bobblysock a lift home in her tractor.

When Mr. and Mrs. Shinyshoes
came home later, Claude and Sir
Bobblysock were tucked up in bed.

"Good gracious!" said Mrs.
Shinyshoes, wafting her hand
around. "There's a frightful whiff in
here! Do you think it's Claude?"

92

Mr. Shinyshoes laughed. "I don't know," he said. "Let's ask him when he wakes up. We can also ask him where on earth this lasso has come from!"

In his bed, Claude smiled a little smile.

Of course he knew where it had come from.

And we do too, don't we?

Keep your eyes open for Claude and Sir Bobblysock.
You never know where they'll turn up next.

CLAUDE:
in the City

A visit to the city is delightful but ordinary until Claude accidentally foils a robbery and heals a whole waiting room full of patients! HC: $12.95 / *978-1-56145-697-0,* PB: $7.95 / *978-1-56145-843-1*

CLAUDE:
at the Circus

An ordinary walk in the park leads to a walk on a tightrope when Claude accidentally joins the circus and becomes the star of the show! HC: $12.95 / *978-1-56145-702-1*

CLAUDE:
at the Beach

A seaside holiday turns out to be more than Claude bargained for when he saves a swimmer, encounters pirates, and discovers treasure! HC: $12.95 / *978-1-56145-703-8*

CLAUDE:
on the Slopes

Claude loves the Snowy Mountains—but when his winter wonderland threatens to avalanche, he must make a daring rescue! HC: $12.95 / *978-1-56145-805-9*

CLAUDE:
in the Spotlight

Claude is ready for his stage debut—but when a spooky theater ghost tries to ruin the performance, Claude knows the show must go on! HC: $12.95 / *978-1-56145-895-0*